CHINA AND JAPAN
BY J. BARTHOLOMEW, F.R.G.S.
English Miles
100 0 100 200 300 400
Treaty Ports thus Swatow
EMPIRE
MANCHURIA
Mongolia
Tsetsen-khan
Sakhalin Island
OKHOTSK SEA
C. Patience
Gulf of Tartary
Blagovestchensk
Khabarovka
Nerchinsk
Chita
Hei-lung-kiang
Tsitsihar
Kirin
Vladivostok
La Perouse Strait
Iturup
Urup
Yesso
Sangar Str.
Tsugaru or
SEA OF JAPAN
Sheng-king
Mukden
Gulf of Pe-chi-li
Pe-chi-li
Korea Bay
KOREA
SEOUL
Chemulpo
Gensan
Broughton Bay
Fusan
Dagelet I.
Oki Is.
HONDO
TOKIO
Yokohama
Kioto
Sado I.
Shikoku
Kiushu
Nagasaki
Korea Strait
Kagoshima
Van Diemen Strait
Tanega Sima
Shan-si
Shan-tung
Kiao-chow
Wei-hai-wei (Br.)
YELLOW SEA
Quelpart I.
Ho-nan
Kiang-su
Shanghai
Ngan-whei
Hu-pe
Hankow
Che-kiang
Ningpo
Chusan Archipelago
TUNG HAI OR EASTERN SEA
Kiang-si
Hu-nan
Fo-kien
Fu-chow
Amoy
Kwang-tung
Canton
Hong Kong & Victoria
(British)
Macao
Tai-wan
Formosa
(Japan)
Tai-nan
South Cape
Pescadores Is.
Fo-kien Strait
Formosa Strait
Tam-sui
Keelung
Majico Sima Group
Riu Kiu or Loo Choo Islands
Chusan or Middle Is.
Linchoten
PACIFIC OCEAN
NAN HAI OR SOUTH CHINA SEA
Hai-nan
Hai-nan Strait
Bashee Is.
Babuyan Is.
C. Engano
Luzon
1&13
2
3
4
5
6
8
10
11
12
110
115
120
125
130
135
140
145
50
40
35
30
25
20
15

CHINESE IMPERIAL POST
Lost and Found
Adèle & Simon in China
Barbara McClintock
Farrar Straus Giroux • New York

大清郵政明信片

Dear Mama,

Simon and I are in Hong Kong! Uncle Sidney met us at the dock. He's taking us shopping for things to buy for our trip with him around China. We are so excited!

Love,
Adèle

右邊只寫收信人名姓住址

Madame Trouvée
36, rue des Morillons
Paris, France

茶莊
鼎興茶莊
元利洋貨布

拾物伏筆店
美術用品
照相機
天籟末聞樂器
服裝店
洋服裁縫
美術用品
寧靜致遠

Dear Mama,
Uncle Sidney bought Simon

a hat,

a jacket,

a knapsack,

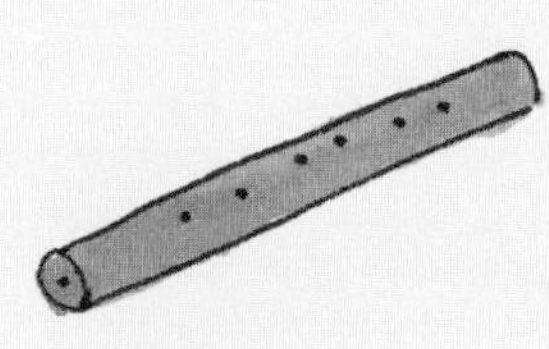

a flute,

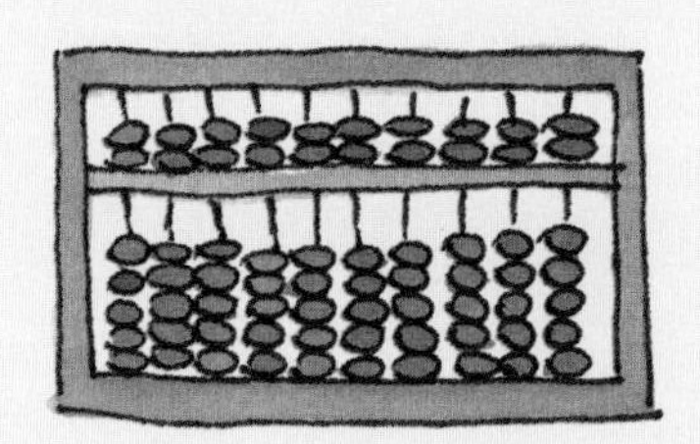

an abacus,

a fan,

a scroll of paper,

a drinking bowl,

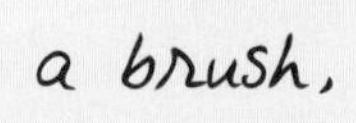

a brush,

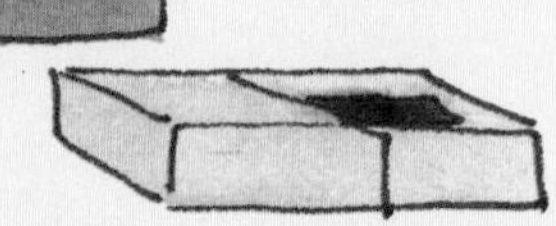

an ink box,

and a scarf.

And for me . . . a camera of my own! Now I can take pictures of everything I see, just like Uncle Sidney does.

When we got to Uncle Sidney's house, he showed us a map of China and all the places we'd be going with him.

We ate dinner,

brushed our teeth,

and went to bed.

Uncle Sidney said we'd need a good night's sleep to be ready for our trip bright and early the next morning.

Love,
Adèle

Dear Mama,
The first stop on our trip was a silk farm near Shanghai. Did you know silk comes from silkworm cocoons? Simon lost his scarf.
Love,
Adèle

Dear Mama,
Today we were in a town that's built on a canal.
There were people carrying all kinds of things on
boats. We ate tiny candied apples on long sticks.
Simon lost his abacus.
Love,
Adèle

Dear Mama,
We were in Peking! We walked by the Forbidden City. We saw vendors selling kites and food. We watched acrobats and musicians. Simon wanted to play along, but he lost his flute.
Love,
Adèle
大聲戲院
院
戲

雙貓茶館
貓茶館
雙貓茶館

Dear Mama,
Today we walked along the
Great Wall. Uncle Sidney
and I took pictures. Simon did
somersaults. It's no surprise that
he lost his hat.
Love,
Adèle

Dear Mama,

Today we visited a family who lives in a tent called a ger. We had hot milk tea in bowls. Simon lost his bowl, but Uncle Sidney let him use his. I would never, ever let Simon touch my bowl! Yuck!

Love,
Adèle

Dear Mama,
We rode across the desert on camels. It sure was hot! Simon lost his fan.
Love,
Adèle

Dear Mama,

The monks in Xi'an showed us how to make brush paintings. Simon lost his brush. I let him use the brush the monks gave me.

Love,
Adèle

Dear Mama,
Today we hiked in a bamboo forest. Simon made a new friend. And he lost his ink box.
Love,
Adèle

Dear Mama,
We met some more monks on top of a mountain. They taught us martial arts! Simon wanted to show them his scroll, but he couldn't find it.
Love,
Adèle

Dear Mama,
Last night,
we watched
fishermen
on a river
use birds
to catch
fish! Simon
lost his
knapsack.
Love,
Adèle

Dear Mama,
We saw fields
wrapped
around
mountains
like giant
ribbons.
Simon lost
his jacket.
Love,
Adèle

Dear Mama,

We finally got back to Uncle Sidney's house.

We developed our photographs.

Guess what? We found all of Simon's lost things in the pictures I took!

Even though the silk farm and canals and acrobats and musicians and Great Wall and gers and camels and pagodas and monks and fishing birds and rice farms were great, it will be good to travel back home to you soon, Mama!

Love,
Adèle

Pages 6–7: Hong Kong
With its deep water and natural shelter between Hong Kong Island and Kowloon, Victoria Harbour was an ideal port for oceangoing trade ships from around the world. The development of the harbor helped Hong Kong become a major trading center in the South China Sea region. Between 1842 and 1997, Hong Kong was part of the British Commonwealth, and the city's culture continues to be a vibrant mix of Chinese and European traditions.

Pages 8–9: Hong Kong
Travelers like Adèle and Simon could find anything they needed in the small street shops in Hong Kong and other cities in China. Stores offered goods ranging from musical instruments, clothing, and art supplies to expensive teas and rare teapots.

Pages 12–13: Hangzhou
Legend has it that in 3000 B.C., Lady Xi Lingshi discovered silk when a moth cocoon dropped into her cup of tea and unraveled into a single gossamer thread. Silk production was a carefully guarded secret in China until approximately 440 B.C. when, according to another legend, a betrothed princess smuggled silk cocoons out of China in her ornate hairpiece.

Silkworms are carefully tended and fed mulberry leaves until they build their cocoons. The silkworm cocoons are steamed or baked, and then dipped into hot water to loosen the tightly woven filaments. Each individual silk cocoon is made of one filament that is almost half a mile long. Several filaments are twisted together to make one silk thread.

Pages 14–15: Tongli
Tongli is an ancient town near the Yangtze River in eastern China. Forty-nine stone bridges cross the city's rivers and canals, the oldest one built during the Song dynasty over 1,000 years ago. The smallest bridge is only about five feet long and less than a meter wide.

Pages 16–17: Peking
The capital city of China was known as Peking in 1905, the year of Adèle and Simon's visit. The Westernized spelling and pronunciation of the name have changed over the city's long history, and the preferred spelling now is Beijing (which means "Northern Capital" in Mandarin, the official language of China). The city has a rich history dating back over 3,000 years. It has been the political center of China for most of the last eight centuries.

Beijing is renowned for its thriving culture of performance and visual arts and crafts. Peking Opera—a form of traditional Chinese theater that combines instrumental music, singing, mime, dance, and acrobatics—evolved in Beijing from the late eighteenth to the early twentieth century. Today, Beijing is one of the most populous cities in the world. It is the capital of the People's Republic of China and continues to be a dominant cultural center.

Pages 18–19: Great Wall
Built to keep invading tribes from the north out of central China, the Great Wall is the longest man-made structure on earth, consisting of over 4,000 miles of stone walls and towers, snaking over rugged mountaintops, spanning deserts, and reaching all the way from the Lop Nur Basin in the west to the Yellow Sea in the east.

Millions of soldiers, peasants, and prisoners were forced to labor on the Great Wall during a succession of imperial dynasties over 2,000 years, primarily between the Qin and Ming dynasties. Workers carried large heavy stones up the mountains on their shoulders and backs. Human chains were also used to pass stone blocks up steep mountain slopes. Many peasants died and are said to be buried inside the wall.

Today, the Great Wall is a popular tourist destination, attracting up to 70,000 visitors a day.

Pages 20–21: Xilinhot
The nomadic tribes of Mongolia live in portable tents called gers. Mongols follow their herds of sheep and goats to grazing grounds according to the seasons. Gers are designed to be easy to assemble and easy to take apart and can be packed on the backs of horses when it is time to move to the next grazing land. There are still nomadic peoples moving across Mongolia, although their numbers today are dwindling.

Pages 22–23: Dunhuang

The Mogao Caves are near Dunhuang, an oasis along the Silk Road in the Gobi Desert. In the year 366, the first caves were dug out of cliffs as places of Buddhist meditation and worship. Over the next 1,000 years, more caves were dug and decorated with colorful murals, statues, textiles, paintings, and images printed on paper.

In the early 1900s, many items were taken from the caves by foreign explorers and dispersed around the world. Beginning in the 1940s, efforts were made to repair and preserve the murals and to look after the site and its contents. Today, the Mogao Caves are a UNESCO World Heritage Site. Ongoing archaeological projects continue to document, preserve, and protect the caves and their valuable artifacts.

Pages 24–25: Xi'an

The Great Wild Goose Pagoda is located in the Buddhist Ci'en monastery near Xi'an, China. The pagoda is a tower-like structure made of brick. Its square floors are large at the base and become smaller with each story stacked on top of the last.

A monk is teaching Simon how to write Chinese calligraphy with a bamboo brush and ink on traditional rice paper. The word *calligraphy* means "beautiful writing." It is a highly regarded form of art as well as a mode of communication in China. How an individual writes is as important as what an individual writes; calligraphy is considered as much a means of self-expression as poetry is. Correct strokes, stroke order, character structure, balance, and rhythm are the components of calligraphy and take much practice to learn.

Pages 26–27: Dazhou

Giant pandas are native to the temperate mountain forests of China, and spend most of their time eating, resting, or seeking food. Their diet consists almost exclusively of bamboo. One panda needs to eat between 26 and 84 pounds of bamboo a day—almost 40 percent of its own weight.

Giant pandas were once widespread across central, southern, and eastern China. Because of habitat loss from deforestation, giant pandas now live in only a few areas in central China and are an endangered species.

Pages 28–29: Wudang Mountains

A complex of monasteries is located high up in the Wudang Mountains in Hubei province, south of Xi'an. It is one of the sacred places of Taoist religious practices, and a place where nuns and monks perfected martial arts techniques. The complex is made up of numerous temples and shrines constructed over the course of several centuries on different elevations ascending the mountains. Some were built on sheer cliff faces; others straddle the tops of mountain ridges.

Students from all over the world travel to the temples to study the Taoist arts—internal alchemy, Chinese medicine, scripture, ceremony, internal martial arts, qigong, tai chi, sword forms, and other martial arts disciplines. The Wudang building complex is a UNESCO World Heritage Site.

Pages 30–31: Li River

For millennia, fishermen in China have used trained cormorants to fish in rivers and lakes. A fisherman ties a snare around the base of the cormorant's neck to prevent the bird from swallowing larger fish. When the cormorant dives underwater and catches a fish, it returns to the surface and allows the fisherman to pull the fish out of its mouth. After the cormorant catches several fish, the fisherman removes the snare from around the bird's throat, and the cormorant dives and catches fish for itself to eat. Competition from commercial fishing practices has made cormorant fishing a dying tradition, now done primarily as entertainment for tourists.

Pages 32–33: Longsheng

In mountainous areas of southern China, the sides of steep hills have been carved out to create narrow flat fields that look like steps going up the mountainsides. Soil stays in place during rain, rather than washing away; the water is contained in terraced pools for planting and propagation. Some terraced fields are thousands of years old. The primary crop grown in terraced fields is rice.

Pages 34–35: Hong Kong

The Brownie camera, created by the Eastman Kodak Company and first sold in 1900, was in common use by 1905. It was a basic, easy-to-use, and inexpensive camera made of cardboard with a simple lens. It used roll film, which was advanced by turning a small lever on the side of the camera. The camera film was developed using a device that made it possible to develop film without a darkroom. The photographs from early Brownie cameras were printed in black-and-white; later Brownie cameras used color film.

The marketing slogan for the Brownie was "You push the button, we do the rest." The Brownie, marketed extensively to children, was named after the beloved characters created by the children's author and illustrator Palmer Cox.

The last Brownie camera was sold in the 1970s. It remains one of the most popular and iconic cameras ever made.

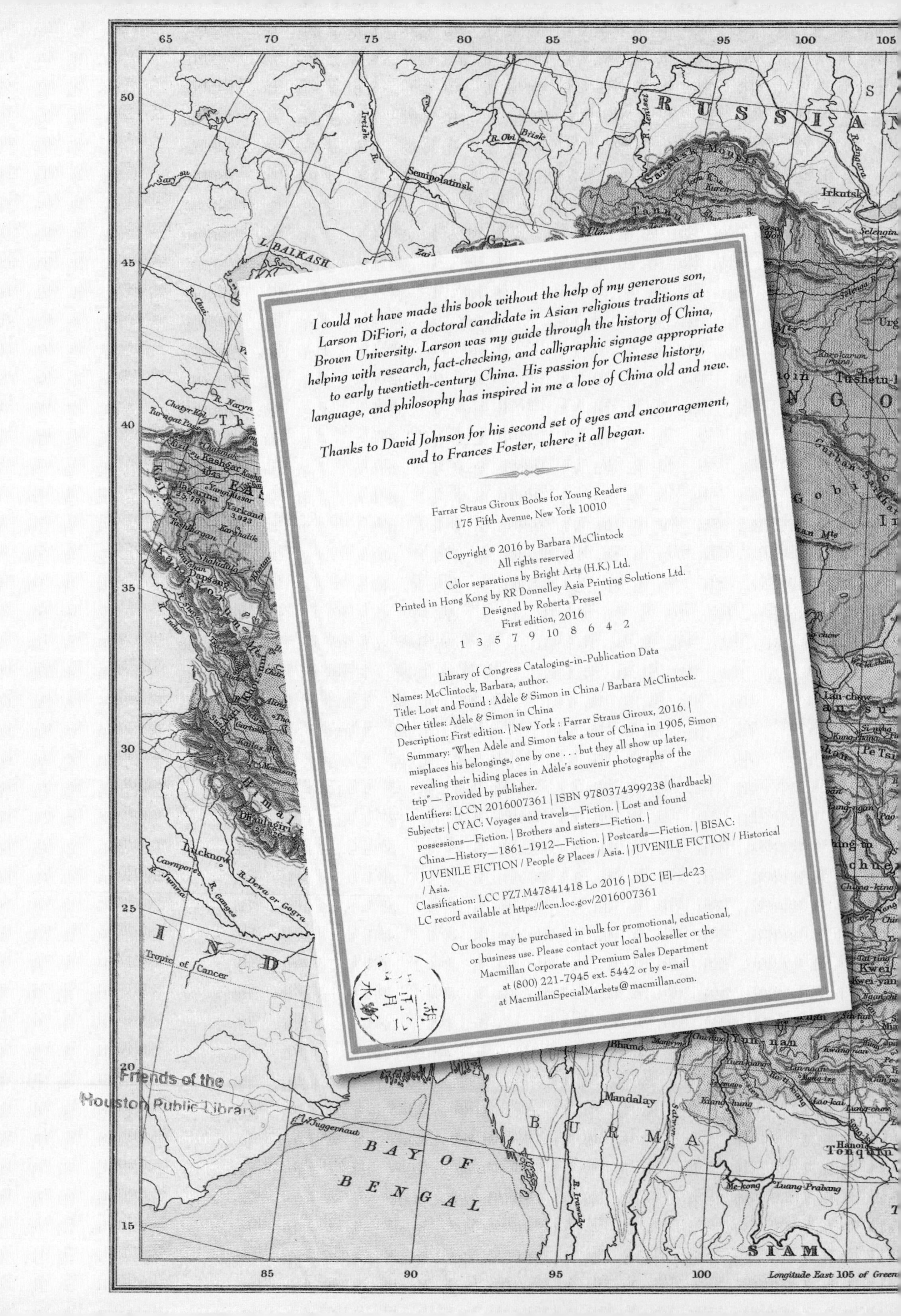

I could not have made this book without the help of my generous son, Larson DiFiori, a doctoral candidate in Asian religious traditions at Brown University. Larson was my guide through the history of China, helping with research, fact-checking, and calligraphic signage appropriate to early twentieth-century China. His passion for Chinese history, language, and philosophy has inspired in me a love of China old and new.

Thanks to David Johnson for his second set of eyes and encouragement, and to Frances Foster, where it all began.

Farrar Straus Giroux Books for Young Readers
175 Fifth Avenue, New York 10010

Color separations by Bright Arts (H.K.) Ltd.
Printed in Hong Kong by RR Donnelley Asia Printing Solutions Ltd.
Designed by Roberta Pressel
First edition, 2016
1 3 5 7 9 10 8 6 4 2

Library of Congress Cataloging-in-Publication Data
Names: McClintock, Barbara, author.
Title: Lost and Found : Adèle & Simon in China / Barbara McClintock.
Other titles: Adèle & Simon in China
Description: First edition. | New York : Farrar Straus Giroux, 2016. |
Summary: "When Adèle and Simon take a tour of China in 1905, Simon misplaces his belongings, one by one . . . but they all show up later, revealing their hiding places in Adèle's souvenir photographs of the trip"— Provided by publisher.
Identifiers: LCCN 2016007361 | ISBN 9780374399238 (hardback)
Subjects: | CYAC: Voyages and travels—Fiction. | Lost and found possessions—Fiction. | Brothers and sisters—Fiction. | China—History—1861–1912—Fiction. | Postcards—Fiction. | BISAC: JUVENILE FICTION / People & Places / Asia. | JUVENILE FICTION / Historical / Asia.
Classification: LCC PZ7.M47841418 Lo 2016 | DDC [E]—dc23
LC record available at https://lccn.loc.gov/2016007361